For Les Girls, who dance and sing
and wear pretty things

First published in Great Britain in 2005 by
Frances Lincoln Children's Books, 4 Torriano Mews,
Torriano Avenue, London NW5 2RZ
www.franceslincoln.com

British Library Cataloguing in Publication Data
available on request

ISBN 1-84507-099-2

Printed in China
9 8 7 6 5 4 3 2 1

Ruby sings the
BLUES

STORY + PICTURES

by Niki Daly

FRANCES LINCOLN CHILDREN'S BOOKS

Ruby was loud... very loud.
When she hollered down the street,
the man on the top floor yelled,
"Keep it down, Loud-mouth! I'm trying to sleep!"

Hi, everybo

The student on the middle floor shouted, "Hey, Boom-box! I can't hear myself think!"

The saxophonist and the jazz singer in the basement looked at each other. "Awesome!" they said.

dy – I'm home!

At home, Ruby's parents tried to stay calm.
"Ruby dear," they said, "do you think you could
be a bit quieter?"

"Just a teensy bit down," said Ruby's father.

"Lovely!" they said. "Now, do you think you can keep it like that?"

But...

In class, Ruby was loud...
...head-splittingly loud.

At playtime, Miss Nightingale spoke gently to Ruby. "Let's pretend that you're a sound-blaster," said Miss Nightingale, pointing to three buttons on Ruby's blouse. "This button is your 'on' button, this one is your 'off' button, and the one in the middle is your volume control."

Miss Nightingale gave Ruby's middle button a twiddle. "Right! Let's hear you, Ruby," she said.

"You are always on, Ruby, and always loud," said Miss Nightingale. "So why don't we turn down the volume a bit?"

Is this better, Miss?

"Much better, Ruby. Now, go and play!" said Miss Nightingale.

Ruby ran outside, turned her volume control right up
and blasted across the playground:

I'm a sou

The other children couldn't bear it. They all turned
round and shouted, "Switch it off, Ruby!
You're hurting our ears!"

No one wanted to play with Ruby.
She was just too loud to have around.

Switched off and sad, Ruby walked home.

No one in the road even knew she had come home.

That whole day, Ruby kept quiet.

Her mum wondered if she was ill.

But Ruby wasn't ill. She had the blues.

When the sax player and the jazz singer didn't hear Ruby upstairs,
they knocked on the door and asked, "What's up, Ruby?"
In a teensy voice, Ruby explained how nobody wanted
to play with her because she was too loud.

"Well, we think you have an awesome voice,"
said Bernard the sax player.
"Yes," said Zelda, "I'd love to teach you how to use it."
"Would you like to learn how to sing, Ruby?" asked her mother.

Awesome!

Ruby's mum smiled. There was nothing wrong with Ruby.

Every day after school,
Ruby took singing lessons
with Bernard and Zelda.
She copied the musical notes
made by Bernard
on his saxophone.

Zelda taught Ruby how to use
her volume control so that
she could sing sharp, zooming notes
like the sounds of the city…

… and gentle, breathy notes
like a cool evening breeze.
Most of all, she taught Ruby
to sing with feeling.

When the man on the top floor
heard Ruby, he said, "What a beautiful voice!"
The student on the middle floor said, "Cool, man!!"
The kids on the block came out and danced on the sidewalk,
chanting, "Go, Ruby, go!" And Bernard looked at Zelda and said,
"Listen, Ruby's singing the blues."

And when Ruby sang
at her school concert, she was...

... well, just AWESOME.

But… once in a while,
when the neighbours least expect it,
she turns it right up…

Hi, everybody

... just to check that her volume control's still working.